The Swashbuckling Storybook

Bloomsbury Publishing, London, Berlin, New York and Sydney
First published in Great Britain in March 2012 by Bloomsbury Publishing Plc
50 Bedford Square, London, WC1B 3DP
THE PIRATES! IN AN ADVENTURE WITH SCIENTISTS!™
™ and © 2012 Sony Pictures Animation Inc.

A CIP catalogue record for this book is available from the British Library

ISBN 978 1 4088 2986 8
Printed in Italy by Lego Spa
1 3 5 7 9 10 8 6 4 2

All papers used by Bloomsbury Publishing are natural, recyclable products made from
wood grown in well-managed forests. The manufacturing processes conform to the
environmental regulations of the country of origin

www.bloomsbury.com
www.thepirates-movie.co.uk

The Swashbuckling Storybook

GIDEON DEFOE

BLOOMSBURY

LONDON BERLIN NEW YORK SYDNEY

MEET THE CAST

The Pirate Captain
Dashing terror of the high seas. His luxuriant beard is one of the seven wonders of the nautical world.

The Pirate with a Scarf
The Captain's Number Two. Keen to avoid adventures where the pirates end up facing certain death.

The Pirate with Gout
Inexplicably proud of his raging gout.

The Albino Pirate
Loves everything about piracy, apart from the tropical sun.

The Surprisingly Curvaceous Pirate

Certainly not a woman disguised as a man, whatever anybody says.

Queen Victoria

Hates pirates the way normal people hate vegetables.

Mister Bobo

A Man-panzee. More of him later.

Polly

A parrot. If you happen to be a parrot expert, you might have spotted that Polly doesn't look much like a parrot at all. None of the pirates is a parrot expert.

The Pirate Captain had an important announcement.

'That's right, lads – I'm going to enter the Pirate of the Year Awards!'

All the pirates cheered and banged their mugs of grog on the table, even though this decision, I'm sorry to say, will prove to be extremely stupid.

'Every time I've entered I've failed to win, so by the sheer law of MATHS I'm bound to win it this year.'

So the pirates sailed to Blood Island – which was shaped exactly like some blood – to fill in the Pirate of the Year entry form.

Normally adventures start with something more exciting than filling in a form, like battling a giant crab or finding an island inhabited by dinosaurs. Not this adventure. (It is too late to take this book back to the shop.)

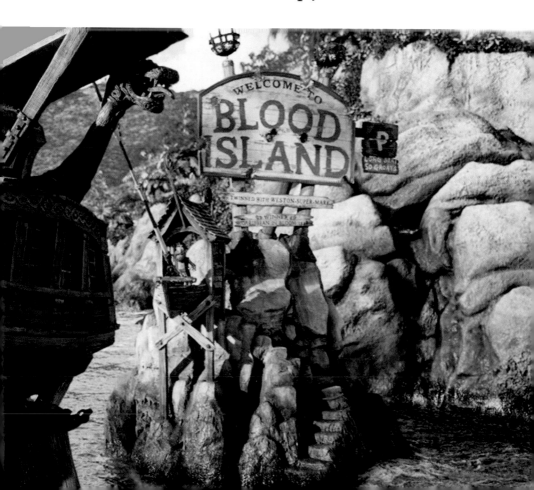

The Blood Island tavern was stuffed full of pirates, all taking a break from plundering things. The Captain sat down and started to fill in the form.

'You can't lose, Captain! I'd bet my face.'

At that moment, with an ear-splitting roar and a shower of glass and splinters, a pirate burst in through the window. Pirates like to make a dramatic entrance.

'It's me, Pegleg Hastings! Back from plundering the Spanish Main!'

He poured a sack of shiny doubloons across the bar. Everybody gasped. But then a huge explosion rocked the tavern.

After the smoke cleared, everybody finished their first gasp and started on a whole new gasp.

There stood Cutlass Liz, who was as beautiful as she was deadly. She tossed away her smoking cannon and sauntered up to the bar.

'Check it out, lubbers – the world's biggest diamond!'

Everybody gasped again. But then the whole room began to shake and an enormous whale burst out of the nearby ocean, belly-flopped on to Blood Island and careened into the tavern with a blubbery smack.

The whale's mouth fell open, and then out stepped a pirate with a neat black beard and a flashy medallion. He surfed a huge wave of gold that spewed from the whale's mouth.

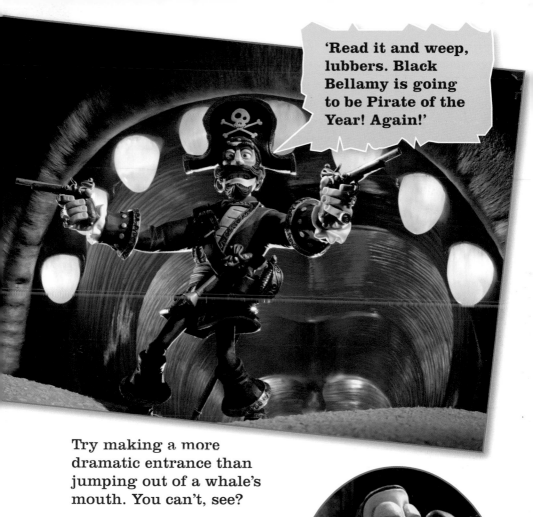

'Read it and weep, lubbers. Black Bellamy is going to be Pirate of the Year! Again!'

Try making a more dramatic entrance than jumping out of a whale's mouth. You can't, see?

The Pirate Captain looked sadly at his tiny bag of booty. He sighed. Then he screwed up the Pirate of the Year entry form and tossed it over his shoulder.

Polly caught the screwed-up bit of paper in mid-air, and started to munch on it.

'Pirate Captain! How's the piracy business treating you? I see you're more wanted than ever!'

The Pirate Captain tried his best to look like he had important things to do and gave Polly an affectionate squeeze.

'I'd love to stay and chat but, you know, places to visit, people to skewer.'

WANTED
PIRATE CAPTAIN

12 DOUBLOONS
REWARD
*AND A FREE PEN!

Polly hiccuped. And wheezed. And then, with a belch, she coughed up the entry form that she had just eaten. It landed right in Black Bellamy's eye.

Bellamy wasn't thrilled. You wouldn't be thrilled if a parrot-who-wasn't-really-a-parrot sicked up a bit of soggy paper on to your face. But when he saw what it was he started to laugh.

'You're entering the Pirate of the Year Awards? AGAIN?'

Cutlass Liz laughed too. So did Pegleg Hastings. Soon everybody in the tavern was laughing. Some of the laughing pirates weren't sure what they were laughing about, but they didn't want to feel left out.

As the laughter rolled on, the Pirate Captain felt himself getting more and more fed up.

'I will be Pirate of the Year! Then you'll all be laughing on the other side of your faces. Which, believe me, is a very painful thing to do.'

The Pirate Captain stormed
back to his boat.

'Come on, lads!
We'll show those
coves a thing or
two about piracy!
Hoist the flag!'

'Standard,
sir?'

'Or extra-gruesome?'

They attacked some boats, because that's pretty much the whole point of being a pirate. Unfortunately, things didn't really go as well as they had hoped.

'Gold? Sorry, old man. This is a leper boat.'

'No gold here. We're naturists, you see.'

'Ghost ship. WOOOOO!'

By the ninth boat the Pirate Captain's eye had started to twitch.

'I'm the Pirate Captain, and I'm here for your gold!'

'I don't think we have any gold. Sorry. This is a scientific expedition. Charles Darwin, at your service.'

The pirate crew tried to cheer him up by getting Darwin to walk the plank.

Darwin was just pondering how sad it was to die without ever having kissed a lady, when he heard a strange 'squawk'. Exactly the sort of squawk a parrot wouldn't make.

'Stop! That bird! She's –' cried Darwin.

But at that point one of the pirates got a bit
carried away, and pushed him off the plank.

'Sorry. It's just . . .
that's my favourite
bit.'

They fished Darwin out of the sea before he
could be nibbled by a shark.

'Polly's not a parrot. She's a dodo. To find
one alive today; it's quite remarkable!
I would be prepared to pay you TEN
POUNDS for her.'

'Polly's not for sale! She's one of the family!'

'She's the feathery heart and soul of the boat.'

'If I could present her at the Royal Society's Science Awards in London, she'd win the top prize!'

The Captain's eyes lit up. Not literally. His eyeballs weren't on fire or anything.

'This prize. Valuable, is it?'

The Captain pulled the face he pulled when he'd had an idea. The Pirate with a Scarf looked worried. When the Captain 'had an idea', it never ended well.

21

'Here's the plan. We go to London. Polly wins this science prize. We take the booty, I enter Pirate of the Year, I win! Bingo!'

'London? The home of Queen Victoria? Mortal enemy to pirates everywhere? We'll end up hanged at Execution Dock!'

22

But once the Captain's mind was made up it was impossible to do anything about it, so they plotted a course for London.

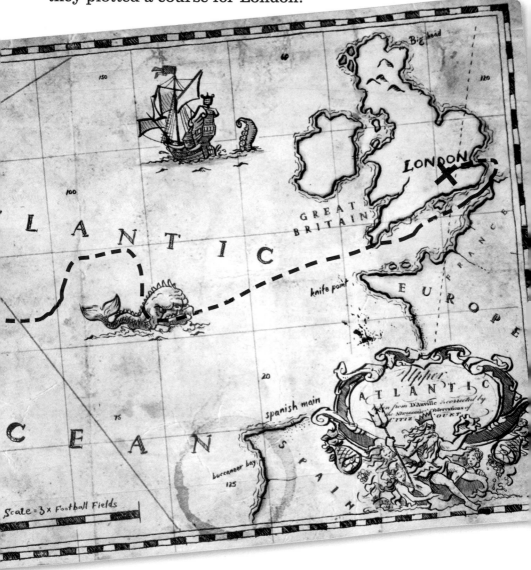

At first the Captain thought it best to avoid the sea monsters drawn on the map, but then Darwin pointed out that they were just added on for decoration.

As they sailed down the Thames they saw a
reassuring sign: Queen Victoria welcomes YOU.
For a moment, the crew really did feel welcome.
Then a monstrous figure lit up and glared at
them: UNLESS YOU'RE A PIRATE.

They parked the boat in the Thames next to Big
Ben. In those days London was a grim place, full
of soot and urchins and people selling jars of fog.

Darwin picked up Polly and started to walk down
the gangplank.

**'I'll bring her back
tomorrow, straight
after the show,'** he said.

**'Don't be daft.
I'll be presenting
Polly,'** said the
Pirate Captain.

Darwin frowned. This wasn't what he wanted at all. He wasn't going to impress anybody with his fantastic dodo discovery if the Pirate Captain took all the credit. He thought fast.

'But London is no place for pirates,' said Darwin.

Not fast enough, as it turned out.

'Pirates? Nobody here but us Girl Guides.'

Darwin took the pirates to his house. When the
door swung open, the pirates got a shock.

'Don't mind Mister Bobo. Just an old
project of mine. The world's first
Man-panzee. Time for bed!'

That night the Pirate Captain dreamt that he'd
won the Pirate of the Year Award. It was a great
dream, until the end, when he started to dream
that someone was trying to steal the award off him.

Except when he woke he
found that there actually
was someone trying to
steal something from him.
A mysterious shadowy figure
was trying to steal Polly!

The pirates gave chase to the mysterious
shadowy figure. They managed to scare
him off and get Polly back, but they did
sort of trash Darwin's house along the
way. This is why people rarely invite
pirates back for tea.

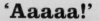

'Aaaaa!'

27

It's good to try to see the best in people, but the Pirate Captain could be a bit too trusting.

'You and your hench-monkey tried to steal Polly!'

'Some jealous rival scientist must have tried to make off with the dodo.'

'Ah. Well, that explains everything.'

Darwin drove them to the Royal Society the next morning.

'Nice going, banana butt. Now this briny buffoon is going to grab all the glory!'

When they reached the awards show, they saw a sign: Scientists Only. Did I mention that the Pirates were masters of disguise? And also, the Pirate Captain was a master of hiding things.

'But where's Polly?'

'Hidden! In case that mysterious shadowy figure should try to make off with her again.'

Darwin said something terrible under his breath, and tried not to look too disappointed.

The pirates waited excitedly for the Pirate Captain to come on stage. A fusty scientist was talking about his new invention, an airship. The pirates preferred regular ships to airships, so they didn't pay much attention. But you should pay attention, because that airship may prove important later on.

Sometimes science presentations can be a bit dull. But the Pirate Captain wasn't dull at all. The Pirate Captain knew how to put on a show.

'Back from the dead! Back from beyond the grave! She's travelled halfway across the globe to be here tonight . . . Heeeerrrre's Polly!'

'By Jove!' 'An actual dodo!' 'Astounding!'

Everybody agreed that a real live dodo was easily the best scientific discovery they had ever seen, even better than electricity.

The Captain wondered whether he'd be able to fit all the priceless booty in his pockets, or whether he'd need a wheelbarrow. He almost didn't notice when the head of the Royal Society presented him with a boring set of leather-bound encyclopedias.

'Where's the priceless prize?'

'It's not all about money. The real prize is a personal audience with Queen Victoria!'

Sometimes a lubber's definition of 'priceless' and a pirate's definition of 'priceless' aren't the same thing at all.

The bugles trumpeted, the doors flew open, and in rode Queen Victoria on a tiny pony. She was very short, and shaped like one of those things some people have to hold toilet rolls.

Nobody said that out loud. You don't say, 'You're shaped like a toilet roll holder' to a queen.

'Where is your dear little dodo?'

'Hidden away, Your Majesty. In case mysterious shadowy figures should try to make off with her.'

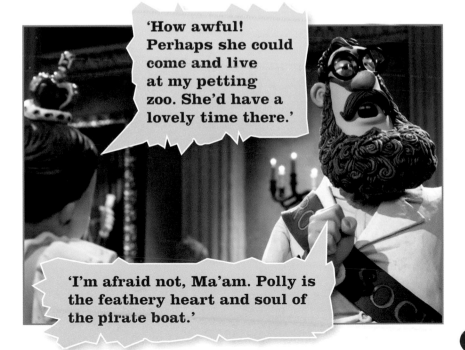

'How awful! Perhaps she could come and live at my petting zoo. She'd have a lovely time there.'

'I'm afraid not, Ma'am. Polly is the feathery heart and soul of the pirate boat.'

Everything stopped.

The Queen frowned.

'Did you say pirate?'

'No! No! Scientist!'

The Pirate Captain tried to look sciency by mixing a couple of test tubes together, but unfortunately this just made his lab coat catch fire. He was having one of those days.

Queen Victoria clicked her fingers, and before the pirates knew what was happening two burly beefeaters were dragging the Pirate Captain towards a big chopping block.

An executioner started to sharpen his axe. The Pirate Captain decided that this hadn't been his most successful adventure ever.

But just before the axe came crashing down on the Captain's neck . . .

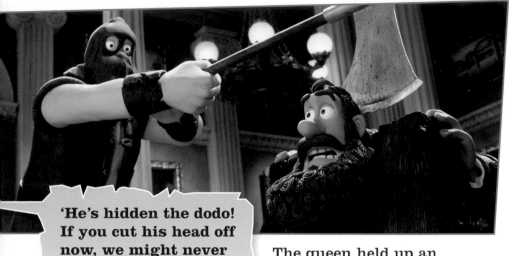

'He's hidden the dodo! If you cut his head off now, we might never find out where!'

The queen held up an imperious hand and smiled a slightly sinister smile.

'One doesn't know why, but one has taken a shine to this pirate. We hereby pardon you of your piratical crimes!'

'You will stay in London, and entertain us with your stories and your wit. And especially with your dear little dodo.'

'I'll get you that dodo, Your Majesty.'

Darwin followed a trail of discarded scientist disguises back to the boat. The pirates wanted to make a sharp exit.

'But you can't go, Captain! You're famous!'

There was a picture of the Pirate Captain on the front page of the newspaper. When you're famous, people suddenly pay attention to you for no good reason. The Captain liked people paying attention to him, so he decided to stay for *just one drink*.

That evening the Captain drank a bit more grog than he should have done, so he was feeling quite tired and emotional. He wobbled a bit.

'The lads all think I'm a joke!'

'No! You're an intellectual giant! Look how brilliantly you kept Polly hidden!'

'Do you want to know where? Ta-da!'

The Captain pulled Polly from his beard.

Darwin narrowed his eyes and nudged Mister Bobo.

The Captain frowned. It's pretty rude when a monkey pulls out a gun and points it at you, even if the monkey is as nicely dressed as Mister Bobo.

Darwin grabbed Polly, and then he and Bobo hared off towards the Tower of London.

Quick as a flash, the Pirate Captain stole a penny-farthing from a passing vicar. (This isn't really acceptable behaviour, but it was an emergency.)

It turns out that a pirate on a penny-farthing is slightly faster than a scientist and a monkey on foot. He caught up with Darwin and Mister Bobo just as they darted inside the Tower of London.

The Captain grabbed Polly back again, and Darwin started to bawl like a baby.

The Captain was a forgiving sort of pirate, so he gave Darwin a handkerchief and patted him on the back.

'Why didn't you say so? We've all done stupid things to impress women.'

'I'm sorry. It's just, there's this girl. I really wanted to impress her.'

'Must be quite a girl, for you to go to all that trouble,' said the Pirate Captain.

Suddenly a light pinged on.

'She IS quite a girl, Captain.'

She jabbed at some buttons, and Darwin and Bobo disappeared through a trapdoor. Darwin might not have behaved very well, but dropping him down a trapdoor seemed harsh.

'What are you playing at, Vicky?'

'I seem to recall you pirates have a soft spot for shiny things.'

She pressed another button and the floor and the wall started to revolve with a mechanical *clunk*.

The floor stopped revolving and the Captain found himself in a huge, glittering treasure room.

There was more booty than he had ever seen. Every kind of jewel you can imagine was piled on top of priceless paintings piled on top of rare stamps piled on top of big gold bricks.

The Captain looked at the treasure. Then he looked at Polly. Then he looked back at the treasure. Then he looked back at Polly.

This was what people call a 'moral dilemma'.

The Captain wasn't very good at moral dilemmas.

Back on the boat, the other pirates were flabbergasted to see the Captain atop a mountain of booty.

'But . . . how?'

'I stole it all from the Tower of London. Then I wrestled a bear and kissed a princess.'

That moral dilemma? You can probably guess what decision he had made.

So the pirates sailed all the way back to Blood Island as fast as they could manage, which was quite fast now they realised they didn't have to avoid the monsters drawn on the map.

The Pirate of the Year Awards was easily the most exciting thing the pirate crew had ever been to in their lives.

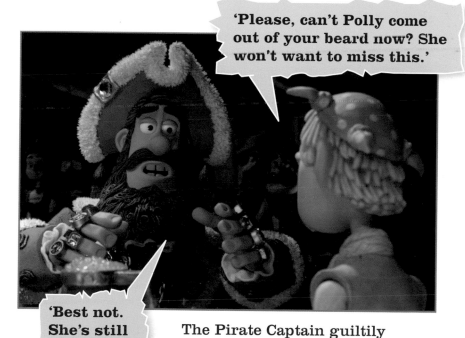

'Please, can't Polly come out of your beard now? She won't want to miss this.'

'Best not. She's still very tired.'

The Pirate Captain guiltily patted his beard.

Out of nowhere, the Pirate King appeared on stage. He leapt out of a giant clam shell and punched a shark. I told you pirates like to make dramatic entrances. The crowd went wild.

'This year's winner is . . . the Pirate Captain!'

Nobody could quite believe it. The Captain's big moment had finally arrived!

Suddenly there was a commotion at the back of the auditorium. Black Bellamy held up a newspaper. There was a picture of the Pirate Captain on the front page.

'Queen Victoria has **PARDONED** the Pirate Captain! And if you've been pardoned . . . well then, technically you're no longer a pirate. So you can't very well be Pirate of the Year, can you!'

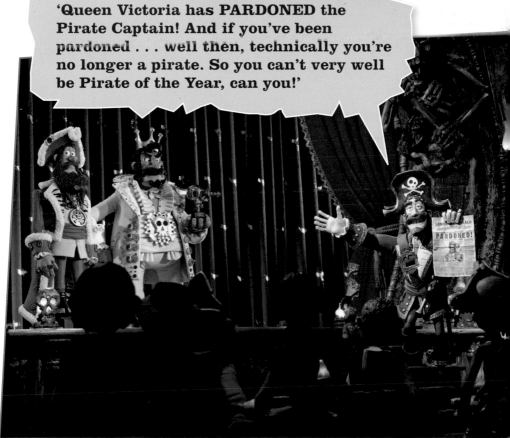

The Pirate King bellowed so loudly that the walls shook and bits of plaster rained down from the ceiling.

'Oh, villainous treachery! Treacherous villainy! You are hereby banished from Blood Island! You are a pirate NO MORE!'

Two burly pirates threw the Pirate Captain out of the theatre. He landed in a puddle. Life has a habit of going from a very good bit to a very bad bit surprisingly quickly.

The other pirates tried to look on the bright side. They thought about all the things they loved about being pirates.

'Shanties!' 'Exotic diseases!' 'Ham!' 'Polly!'

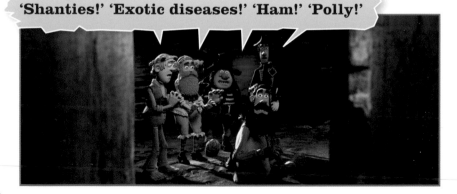

'Where IS Polly?'

'I sold her to Queen Victoria for a boatload of treasure.'

The pirate crew gasped. A few of their lips started to wobble.

'Don't look so upset. She'll be having a lovely time in the Queen's petting zoo!'

But it was no good. Imagine if somebody sold your favourite pet or best friend to buy a new car. Well, that's how the pirates felt. They trudged away from the Pirate Captain, feeling more miserable than they could ever remember feeling.

'Fine! Go on then! It's not like I need any of you anyway!'

The Captain hitched a lift back to London, because he couldn't think where else to go now he didn't have any treasure, or any crew, or even a boat.

He hoped that the Victorians who'd been interested in him when he was in the newspaper might still want to be friends. But nobody really cared any more.

That's the danger of people only liking you because you're famous.

He moped about and generally felt very sorry
for himself. Then one day, mid-mope, he
suddenly realised that really he had done a
pretty terrible thing.

And it needed to be put right.

The Pirate Captain crept into Queen Victoria's
petting zoo, and tiptoed towards the dodo enclosure.
But Polly's cage was empty.

'Oh, it's too terrible. Queen Victoria doesn't want Polly for her petting zoo at all.'

'Darwin? Is that you?'

Darwin had discovered that Queen Victoria was a member of a terrible secret dining society. Every year, rulers from around the world met on her flagship, the *QV1*, to eat the most endangered animals they could find. This year they were going to eat . . . dodo!

Darwin started to snivel but the Pirate Captain grabbed him by his coat.

'We've got to rescue her! Are you with us, Mister Bobo?'

But Mister Bobo had already gone. Then the Captain had a bright idea.

'To the airship!'

I told you the airship was going to be important.

'Nothing! Where the devil can she be?'

They bobbed across the sky, and the Pirate Captain scanned the ocean for any sign of the *QV1*. He was so busy looking in the wrong direction, they almost crashed into it.

Unfortunately the airship didn't come with an anchor, so the Captain decided to use Darwin instead.

'This might sting a bit, Chuck. Try to grab hold of something.'

They'd got to the *QV1* without a moment to spare, because the Rare Creatures Dining Club was just finishing off the first course.

'How do you like my pygmy elephant nuggets, Your Majesty?'

'They're good. But not quite RARE enough for my tastes.'

'Gaston! I think we're ready for the main course.'

The kitchen was the size of a football pitch, full of knives and ovens and boiling pans of water. Generally a pretty bad place to be if you were food.

The chef picked up Polly by the scruff of her neck and licked his lips.

'Come on my pretty, eet ees time to be delicious!'

THWACK.

'I'm sorry, old girl! I'll never leave you again!'

Suddenly Queen Victoria's voice wafted out of the speaking tube.

'Gaston? Are you there?'

'You know, zee dodo ees a very fattening dish. Eet will go straight to your chubby thighs. A minute on zee lips, a lifetime on zee hips . . .'

The Pirate Captain used his best French accent. He was enjoying himself so much that he didn't notice what was going on behind him.

'Mister Darwin! And the idiotic pirate man again!'

'Come on, Vicky. It's just you, a tiny queen, against me, a dashing terror of the high seas!'

Sometimes people have unexpected skills that you would never guess just from looking at them. For example, the Albino Pirate could fit more than twenty whelks in his mouth at once.

Unfortunately for the Pirate Captain, the Queen's unexpected skill was that she was amazing at fighting. She whirled about like a ninja.

The Pirate Captain didn't stand a chance. Pretty soon he was helplessly wrapped up in sausages.

The Queen plonked Polly on a chopping board and picked up a big knife . . .

But then a hairy arm swung past, and plucked
Polly up and into the air.

This is what they call 'arriving in the nick of time'.
If you're going to turn up to save the day, try not
to leave it quite this late, because it gives people
palpitations.

The Pirate with a
Scarf threw the
Captain a cutlass,
which was a
stupid thing to do.
Luckily the Captain
caught it. He cut
his way free from
the sausages, and
bounded towards
the Queen.

He cut through a rope, and several gigantic barrels crashed down on top of Victoria.

They knocked her off her feet and sent her tumbling down a chute. Darwin bolted the door behind her.

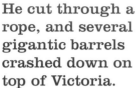

'Sorry, Vicky! Dodo's off the menu!'

'Number Two! You single-handedly took on Queen Victoria's flagship. That's terrifically idiotic. It's also the reason you're the best pirate on the seven seas.'

The Pirate with the Scarf explained that Mister Bobo had rowed halfway across the ocean to tell the pirate crew what the Captain and Darwin were up to.

All the crew cheered. It was hard to stay cross with the Captain for long. After all, he really did have an incredibly luxuriant beard.

Unfortunately the adventure wasn't quite over . . .

The barrels the Captain had knocked over were full of vinegar. And the larder was full of baking powder. If you know anything about chemistry you'll realise that when vinegar and baking powder mix, the results are what scientists technically call 'a right mess'.

A great big wall of foam burst from the larder, carrying Queen Victoria on top of it. She grabbed Polly as she zoomed past.

Soon the foam was everywhere. Rivets popped. Doors buckled. Walls bulged.

The *QV1* was supposed to be unsinkable. But when people claim something is unsinkable it's usually exactly the opposite.

Sure enough, as the wave of foam went on expanding, the *QV1* cracked clean in two and started to sink.

Queen Victoria leapt into the balloon and untied
the rope. She bobbed up into the air.

'Kiss your beaky little
friend goodbye!'

The Captain managed to grab hold of the rope. He inched his way up towards the basket.

Queen Victoria raised Polly to her royal gob. She wasn't going to let anything get in the way of her eating the last dodo in the world. She'd swallow her whole if she had to.

But at that moment Polly pecked her right in the eyeball.

If you've ever been pecked in the eyeball by a
dodo, you'll know that it hurts. Queen Victoria
yelped, jumped backwards . . . and let go of Polly.

Polly started to drop like a feathery rock.
It wouldn't have been a problem for a parrot. But
dodos can't fly.

Fearlessly, the Captain swung across to catch her. Unfortunately the combined weight of a Pirate Captain (who had eaten a lot of feasts in his time) and a dodo (a naturally big-boned bird) was slightly too much for the rope.

'Oh, barnacles.'

As they tumbled towards the *QV1*'s propeller, the Captain's life flashed before his eyes. Most of his life, it turned out, had involved eating ham. He hoped that being mashed into little pieces wasn't going to be as painful as it looked like it might be. He closed his eyes.

Then, a minute later, he opened them again. He was surprised to find all the various bits of him still seemed to be attached to all the other various bits of him.

'Well done, Sir.'

Everybody cheered.
Well, not quite everybody.

'You'll pay for this, Pirate Captain! You'll be outlawed across the globe! There'll be a higher price on your head than any pirate before you!'

It was the best news the Pirate Captain had heard in ages.

Not only was he now the most wanted pirate on the seven seas, the crew even made him a copy of the Pirate of the Year Award.

They made it out of an old cereal box, a bit of squid tentacle and some of the Albino Pirate's earwax, so it wasn't really worth anything, but still. It's the thought that counts.

And with that, the pirate boat sailed off in search of adventure.

THE END